this book belongs to:

Ms. Carter

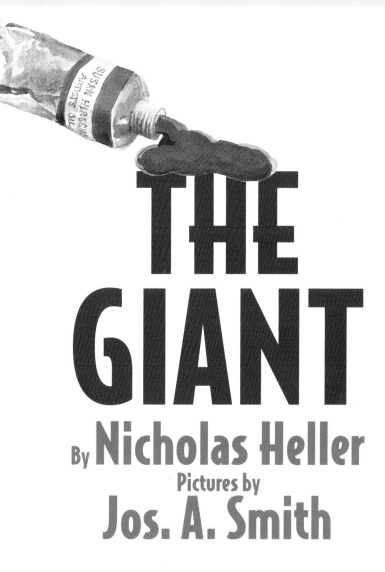

THE GIANT

By Nicholas Heller
Pictures by
Jos. A. Smith

Greenwillow Books, New York

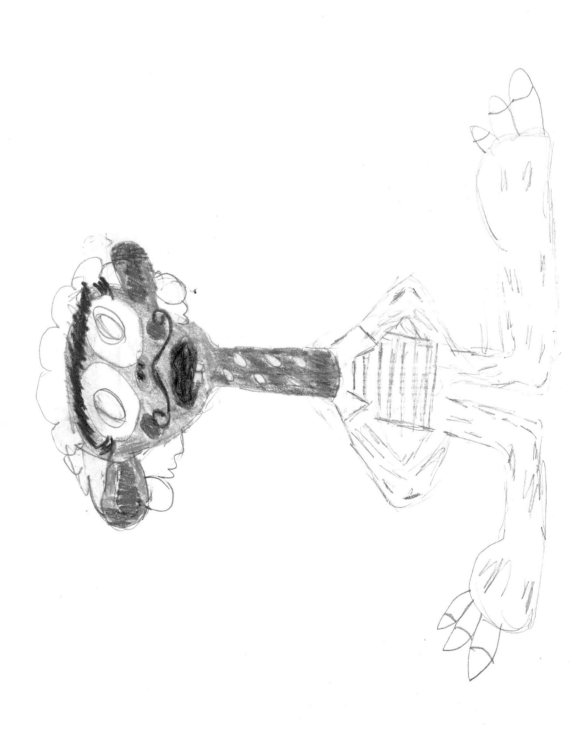

On the west wall of Mrs. Bell's living room, above the green sofa, hung a painting of a giant. It was the most realistic-looking giant that anyone had ever seen, positively bursting with life and energy and looking as though he was quite ready to jump off the canvas onto Mrs. Bell's carpet.

This is just what the giant did, late one Saturday night.

Mrs. Bell's grandson, Evan, who was staying for the weekend, heard the loud thump as the giant landed on the floor. Evan hopped right out of bed and went to investigate.

Of course, he didn't realize at first that the noise had been caused by the giant. But when he got to the living room and shined his flashlight around, Evan noticed the painting and saw that the giant was no longer in it. He also noticed (or rather felt, because it was winter) that the living-room window was wide open. Josephs must have got out that way, he said to himself.

Evan called the giant Josephs after his substitute teacher, Mrs. Josephs. She was large and had the same fierce, slightly bewildered expression as the giant. This was especially true when Mrs. Josephs was angry, which was often. She didn't understand how to control Evan's third-grade class the way their regular teacher did.

Evan shined his flashlight out the window. Sure enough, there were footprints leading away through the snow toward the woods.

Evan noticed that the footprints started out quite small and grew bigger the farther away they went. This was the opposite of the way it should be. Josephs must be growing to his full size, he thought.

Evan felt quite strongly that he should do something, but he had no idea what. He certainly had no desire to follow a giant whom he knew very little about into the woods at night, so he shut the window and went back upstairs to bed.

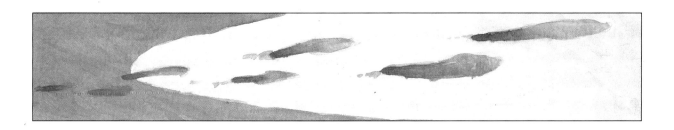

During breakfast Evan heard his grandmother give a startled gasp from the living room, where she had gone in search of her reading glasses.

"Oh, Grandma," Evan called. "The giant got away last night. I heard him!"

Evan ran into the living room to show his grandmother the footprints, but unfortunately it had snowed some more since last night, and they had all been covered up.

"I saw them, though," Evan assured her, and there was certainly no denying the fact that the giant was no longer in the painting. "What should we do, Grandma?" he asked.

Mrs. Bell sat down on the sofa. "Well," she said, fanning herself with a magazine, "I'm not quite sure. Nothing like this has ever happened before. Perhaps," she said after a moment, "it might be a good idea to get in touch with the artist."

"Weller, right?" said Evan, reading the signature at the bottom of the giantless painting. "Do you know him?"

"I met him when I bought the painting," said Mrs. Bell. "Ignatius Weller. An odd character, I seem to recall. Bring me the telephone book, and we'll see if he is listed."

They found the number, and Evan listened in on the extension.

"Mrs. Bell? Dear me," said Ignatius Weller. "I've been afraid that you would be calling. It's about the giant, right? I never should have sold you that painting. You had better come over at once, and please bring the painting with you!"

"This is exciting, isn't it?" said Mrs. Bell a little while later as they were getting into the car.

During the drive Evan kept a sharp eye out for Josephs, but he saw no sign of him.

Ignatius Weller lived about a half hour away in an old farmhouse with an attached barn just like the one in the painting. He was waiting nervously on the front porch and ushered them inside immediately.

"Call me Iggy," he said. "I knew I shouldn't have sold you that painting," he told Mrs. Bell again, "but you seemed to like it so much."

"I do like it," said Mrs. Bell. "At least, I did when the giant was still in it. But how on earth did he get out?"

"Well, you see," Iggy said, "I dreamed him up one night, and in the morning there he was. I mean, there he *really* was, sitting in my backyard, and he was terribly hungry. I gave him all the food I had in the house, but it wasn't enough. And he wouldn't go away. . . . So to get rid of him, I painted him into a picture. But he's gotten out again. I thought he might."

"Hmmm," said Mrs. Bell thoughtfully. "Do things like this happen to you often?"

"Oh, no!" said Iggy, shaking his head vigorously.

Just then the kitchen door swung open and a five-foot-tall pigeon came waddling into the room. It blinked at them and then went straight to the counter and stuck its beak into a cracker box.

"Er," said Iggy, looking quite embarrassed, "now and then, I suppose. But I always paint them into pictures," he added brightly, "and they go away. At least, they're supposed to go away."

"What about him?" said Evan, nodding in the direction of the pigeon.

"Um, I've been meaning to paint him, but I've sort of gotten used to having him around. You should see my barn, though. It's full of paintings. Some of them are really quite extraordinary. I would show you right now, but . . ."

"But?" prompted Mrs. Bell.

"He's out there right now," mumbled Iggy.

"The giant?" asked Evan.

Iggy nodded.

"Then you can paint him back into Grandma's picture, can't you?"

"Exactly!" cried Iggy enthusiastically. "That's why I asked you to bring the painting along. You do have it, don't you?"

"It's in the car," said Evan. "I'll go get it."

Evan kept a sharp eye on the barn as he trotted to the car. He got the painting off the back seat and, as he slammed the door, saw a large eye appear at the hayloft window and stare down at him. Evan hurried back into the house.

"Here it is," he said.

"Good. I'll get to work at once," said Iggy, reaching for the painting. "My paints are already out in the barn."

"What guarantee is there," asked Mrs. Bell sternly, "that the giant will stay in the picture this time?"

"Well, er, they usually do," said Iggy hopefully.

"But not always," said Mrs. Bell.

"No," he admitted.

"Can I come watch?" asked Evan.

"The giant isn't dangerous, is he?" asked Mrs. Bell.

"I wouldn't think so," said Iggy. "I never dream dangerous things, only inconvenient ones. Why don't you both come along?"

The giant glared fiercely at them as they came through the barn door, but he made no move in their direction. If anything, he hunched himself farther into the corner where he was sitting.

"Hiya, Josephs!" Evan called. He thought he saw a faint smile flicker across the giant's face, but his head was in the shadows, and Evan couldn't be sure.

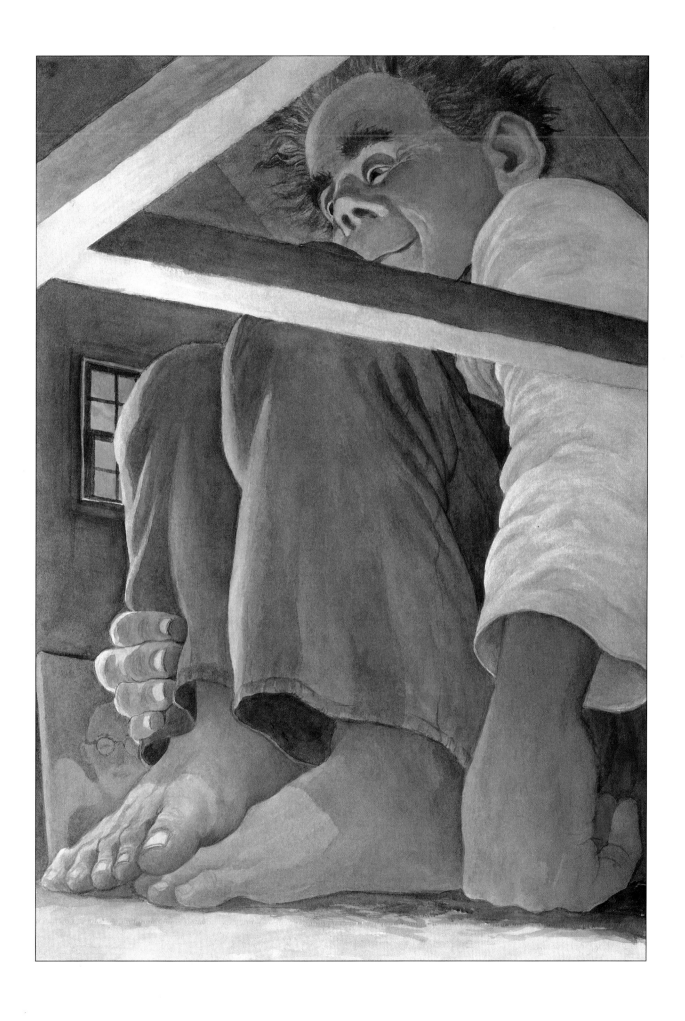

Iggy placed the painting on an easel that was standing in the middle of the floor and then squeezed some paint onto his palette. He worked quickly and expertly, first sketching in the giant's outline with some reddish brown paint, then modeling the individual features with white, yellow, pink, and several shades of tan.

Evan looked back and forth from the painting to the giant huddled uncomfortably in the corner. Yes! As Josephs began to take shape on the canvas, he was fading in real life. Soon you could see right through bits of him to the barn wall behind.

"Look, Grandma!" Evan whispered.

Mrs. Bell nodded. She was watching intently.

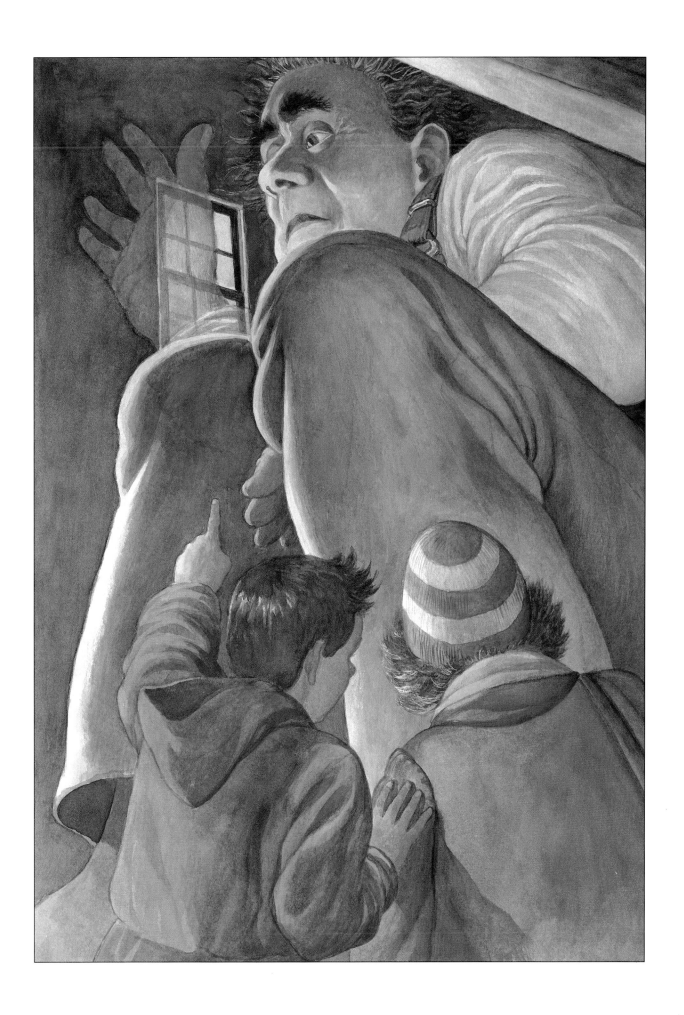

In a short while the giant's head, arms, hands, and enormous feet were finished. Only his body and legs, clad in a massive pair of dirty overalls, remained seated in the corner of the barn.

Iggy roughed in the folds and creases of the fabric with some dark gray, then reached for a new tube of paint and squirted a large blob of bright lavender onto his palette.

"What's that for?" asked Evan.

"His overalls," answered Iggy. "I'm giving him stripes, just as he had before."

It was true that in the original painting the giant had been wearing a striking pair of purple-striped overalls, but the real giant, or what was left of him, had on dirty, worn-out brown ones.

"When you first dreamed him," Evan asked, "was he wearing striped clothes?"

"Oh, no," said Iggy. "But look how dingy the brown ones are. I think he looks so much nicer in the purple-striped, don't you?"

Evan frowned, then he clapped his hands together in excitement. "That must be it!" he shouted.

"That's what?" asked Iggy, dipping a brush into the paint.

"The problem," said Evan. "Don't you see? If you don't paint the giant exactly the way he looks, it gives him a way to get back out of the painting!"

"Hmmm," said Iggy, rubbing his chin and leaving a streak of purple paint on it.

"It makes sense to me," said Mrs. Bell. "As much sense as any of this," she added.

"You could be right," said Iggy thoughtfully. "Do you see that painting there?"

He pointed to a picture leaning against the barn wall, the outermost of a large stack. It showed a grassy field, a clear blue sky, and a blazing sun.

"There used to be a giant frog there," said Iggy. "I added sunglasses when I painted him, and he got away several weeks ago."

"Do you always dream about giants?" asked Mrs. Bell.

"Of course not," said Iggy. "There was that little banana man. I had to chase him all over the house as I was painting his picture. I painted him some lovely jogging shoes. He's gone, too."

Iggy scraped off the lavender paint that he had begun to put on the canvas and finished the giant's overalls with brown, just the way they looked. As he completed his last brush stroke, the real giant faded away completely.

Iggy handed the painting to Mrs. Bell. "This should be all right now," he said. "Just be careful not to bump it until the paint dries."

As Evan and his grandmother were getting into their car for the drive home, Iggy said, "Wait a minute!"

He ran back into the house and returned a few minutes later carrying a small package.

"This is for you, Evan," he said. "I'm really very grateful to you for solving my problem. I suppose I should have figured it out myself, but I've just never been very practical."

Evan unwrapped the package on the way home. It was, as he had suspected, a painting.

For KATE and HANNAH
—N. H.

For
CHARISSA,
KARI and PAUL/ERIC,
NOMI and JOE,
EMILY and ANDREA
—J. A. S.

Watercolor paints and graphite pencils
were used for the full-color art.
The text type is Goudy Sans Medium.
Text copyright © 1997 by Nicholas Heller
Illustrations copyright © 1997 by Jos. A. Smith
All rights reserved. No part of this book may be reproduced or
utilized in any form or by any means, electronic or mechanical,
including photocopying, recording, or by any information storage and
retrieval system, without permission in writing from the Publisher,
Greenwillow Books, a division of William Morrow & Company, Inc.,
1350 Avenue of the Americas, New York, NY 10019.
Printed in Singapore by Tien Wah Press
First Edition 10 9 8 7 6 5 4 3 2 1

Library of Congress Cataloging-in-Publication Data

Heller, Nicholas.
The giant / by Nicholas Heller ;
pictures by Jos. A. Smith.
p.   cm.
Summary: When the giant in a painting in his grandmother's
living room comes alive and walks out of the house, Evan goes
with her to visit the artist and get the giant back into the painting.
ISBN 0-688-15224-4 (trade).   ISBN 0-688-15225-2 (lib. bdg.)
[1. Giants—Fiction.   2. Artists—Fiction.   3. Grandmothers—Fiction.]
I. Smith, Joseph A. (Joseph Anthony), (date) ill.   II. Title.
PZ7.H432132Gi   1997   [E]—dc21
96-36886   CIP   AC

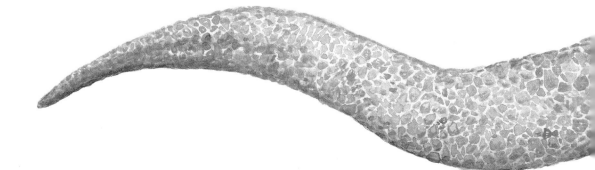